## Learning to Read, Step by Step!

**Ready to Read** Preschool–Kindergarten
• big type and easy words • rhyme and rhythm • picture clues
For children who know the alphabet and are eager to begin reading.

**Reading with Help** Preschool–Grade 1
• basic vocabulary • short sentences • simple stories
For children who recognize familiar words and sound out new words with help.

**Reading on Your Own** Grades 1–3
• engaging characters • easy-to-follow plots • popular topics
For children who are ready to read on their own.

**Reading Paragraphs** Grades 2–3
• challenging vocabulary • short paragraphs • exciting stories
For newly independent readers who read simple sentences with confidence.

**Ready for Chapters** Grades 2–4
• chapters • longer paragraphs • full-color art
For children who want to take the plunge into chapter books but still like colorful pictures.

**STEP INTO READING®** is designed to give every child a successful reading experience. The grade levels are only guides. Children can progress through the steps at their own speed, developing confidence in their reading, no matter what their grade.

Remember, a lifetime love of reading starts with a single step!

*For Andrew*
*—A.J.H.*
*To Super Sosha and Silly Bob*
*—S.W.*

Text copyright © 2002 by Anna Jane Hays.
Illustrations copyright © 2002 by Sylvie Wickstrom.
All rights reserved under International and Pan-American Copyright Conventions. Published in the United States by Random House Children's Books, a division of Random House, Inc., New York, and simultaneously in Canada by Random House of Canada Limited, Toronto.

www.stepintoreading.com

Educators and librarians, for a variety of teaching tools, visit us at
www.randomhouse.com/teachers

*Library of Congress Cataloging-in-Publication Data*
Hays, Anna Jane.
Silly Sara : a phonics reader / by Anna Jane Hays ; illustrated by Sylvie Wickstrom.
   p.   cm. — (Step into reading. A step 2 book)
SUMMARY: Alliterative rhyming tale of a girl who can be very silly but with her best friend, Sam, discovers she can be something more.
ISBN 0-375-81231-8 (trade) — ISBN 0-375-91231-2 (lib. bdg.)
[1. Clumsiness—Fiction.   2. Best friends—Fiction.   3. Stories in rhyme.]
I. Wickstrom, Sylvie, ill.   II. Title.   III. Series: Step into reading. Step 2 book.

PZ8.3.H3337 Sj   2003
[E]—dc21
2002013402

Printed in the United States of America   20 19 18 17

STEP INTO READING, RANDOM HOUSE, and the Random House colophon are registered trademarks of Random House, Inc.

STEP INTO READING®

STEP 2

# Silly Sara

## A Phonics Reader

by Anna Jane Hays
illustrated by Sylvie Wickstrom

Random House 🏠 New York

Sara sat on a sofa.

She sipped a smoothie.

OOPS!

The smoothie spilled.

Silly Sara.

Sara sat in the tub.

She licked a lollipop.

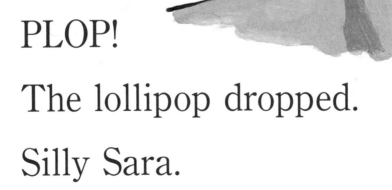

PLOP!

The lollipop dropped.

Silly Sara.

Silly Sara sat
on her hat.

Silly Sara tripped
on her cat.

Silly Sara slipped
on the mat.

Silly Sara missed
with the bat.

Sara chewed
bubble gum.

She blew a big bubble.

Then a bigger bubble.

Then the biggest bubble.

Silly Sara.

The door went SLAM!

In came Sam.

"You have a funny face."

"Hey, want to race?"

Sam and Sara

scooted fast.

Sara was first.

Sam was last.

Speedy Sara!

Sam and Sara played
hide-and-seek.
Sara had to peek.

"Eek!"

Sara saw Sam.

Sam and Sara sat
on a seesaw.
They licked ice cream.

Sandy stepped on.

Sara went up.

Sara's ice cream

fell down.

SLURP!
Sandy found it
on the ground.

Sara had a hunch
it was time for lunch.

Sara had jam.

Sam had ham.

Which?

Sara and Sam had

a jam ham sandwich.

Sam gobbled up his
jam ham sandwich.

"I am Super Sam!"

he said.

"Now <u>you</u> have

a funny face," said Sara.

"Don't be silly, Sara."

"Okay," she said.

"I am not Silly Sara."

"I am <u>Super</u> Sara!"

"And we are super pals!"